Published by Waldorf Publishing

2140 Hall Johnson Road

#102-345

Grapevine, Texas 76051

www.WaldorfPublishing.com

The One Eyed Pug

ISBN: 978-1-945175-78-7

Library of Congress Control Number: 2016957020

Copyright © 2017

The One Eyed Pug

by Deborah Hunt

WALDORF PUBLISHING

Chapter 1 - page 1
The Little Pug

Chapter 2 - page 4
The Farewell Party

Chapter 3 - page 10
An Adventure in the Sky

Chapter 4 - page 13
The New Home

Chapter 5 - page 17
A Forever Home

Chapter 6 - page 22
The Terrible Horrible Thing

Chapter 7 - page 25
The Doctor's Visit

Chapter 8 - page 28
The Dog Park

Chapter 9 - page 31
The Injury

Chapter 10 - page 34
A Trip to the Vet

Chapter 11 - page 36
The Operation

Chapter 12 - page 39
The Road to Recovery

Chapter 13 - page 42
Time to Go Home

Chapter 14 - page 45
The Reunion

CHAPTER 1

The Little Pug

Hi, my name is Lola, and boy do I have a story for you. Now I'll warn you in advance that this is not your typical story, so I suggest you find a comfy spot, and settle in for a truly intriguing tale.

Once upon a time there was a lovely, little pug puppy, who was born in Michigan. She had soft, beige fur, a tiny black face, and a curly tail. Her doggie mother had too many puppies and couldn't take care of all of them. So the lovely little pug puppy was adopted and went to live with a different kind of mommy. Her new mom was named Julie, and she was human. She talked funny and made all sorts of silly faces. She gave the little pug puppy lots of love, bought her a special bed, and lots of toys. Some days the little pug missed her doggie family. But, she did love her new home and hoped that she would stay here forever. Sometimes her new mommy, Julie, would take her to Mrs. Barry's house where her doggie parents, Sasha and Rex, lived with her baby brother Rocky. The little pug loved these visits. All of her siblings would visit at the same time so they could play in the big giant yard.

Then suddenly one day her mother told her that they had to move to New York because she was starting a new job. This was a very exciting time. But it was also kind of scary, and the little pug was sad because she was going to be moving so far away from her doggie family.

"Arf, Arf! Whimper! Whimper!" said the little pug.

"I know you're sad," said Julie. "Please don't worry we're going to have such a great adventure, and maybe your doggie family will be able to visit you in New York."

Wow, that would be cool, thought the little pug. She started to feel a bit better, and when she fell asleep, she dreamt of her doggie family coming to visit her in the big city.

The next few weeks were very busy. There were so many things to do. The little pug had to help Mommy Julie pack all of her clothes, favorite toys, and special blanket.

"Oops, I almost forgot," said Julie. "Most of our things are being sent in the moving van, so we'll need to pack a small bag to take on the airplane."

Airplane! Yikes, I have never been on a plane before, thought the little pug and then ran and hid in her crate.

Her mother sat on the floor and poked her head in the crate. "I know going on an airplane sounds scary, but it's actually cool, and I'll be with you the entire time."

The little pug jumped right into her lap and gave her a bunch of kisses. Then she ran and got her favorite stuffed bear. After playtime, they went out for a nice long walk. Then her mommy said it was time for bed because tomorrow was a very special day.

CHAPTER 2

The Farewell Party

The little pug woke up and ran downstairs to find her mother, but she wasn't there. *Oh my, where's my Mommy? Did she leave without me?* The little pug ran all around the house. She was getting very scared and thought she missed the plane ride.

"I'm back! Did you miss me?"

Hurray! I knew she wouldn't leave without me, the pug thought to herself.

The little pug jumped into her mother's arms and starting licking her all over.

Mommy laughed. "I missed you too, but now we have to hurry so we won't miss our farewell party."

The little pug loved lots of things, but parties were her favorite.

And this one was super special because everyone was going to be there to wish them well. The pug's doggie family, her dog walker, the dog groomer, and all of her mommy Julie's family were coming. The party was at Mrs. Barry's house where she had been born. Her mommy, daddy, and baby brother Rocky still lived there. It was a great big house with a giant yard so they could all run around and play their favorite games.

It was a beautiful sunny day. The backyard was filled with people and puppy dogs. There were even a few cats, a couple of rabbits, and a very outspoken colorful parrot. There were tons of balloons, party streamers, toys, and two giant tables filled with food. One was for the humans, and the other for the pets.

When the pug puppy and her human mommy walked into the yard everyone cheered. "Hip hip hooray, we're going to have a great day!"

"Mommy, Mommy I missed you so much." The little pug started to cry when she spotted her doggie mommy.

Her doggie mother rubbed her and gave her a bunch of kisses. "I missed you too! I love you so much, but I know your mommy Julie loves you too! Right now she needs you to be very brave. Now go play and have fun, and we'll talk again later."

The little pug ran over to her brothers, sisters, cousins, and friends who were all playing a game of tag. It was great fun. Of course, the parrot was winning because he could just fly away when anyone got too close.

"The food is all ready," said Mrs. Barry. "Everyone please help yourselves and enjoy. After dinner, our guests of honor can open presents, and then we'll have the yummy cakes."

Presents! she thought. The little pug was excited. *Maybe moving wasn't going to be so bad after all.*

There was so much good food. Everyone just ate, and ate, and ate some more. The little pug wished everyone would hurry up so she could open her gifts.

"Okay, everyone gather round," said Mrs. Barry.

Everyone sat in a big circle and watched the little pug and Julie open the colorful packages. "There's one more," said Mrs. Barry who pointed to a box covered in purple paper and pink bows.

The little pug tore off the paper and pushed open the lid. She looked inside. All of the sudden, she started to cry and took off toward the other side of the yard.

"What's wrong? We thought you would like our surprise. We never meant to upset you," said her doggie mommy.

"Having a picture of my doggie family is the best present in the whole wide world. I'm just sad because I'm going to miss you all so much," cried the little pug.

"We're going to miss you too," said her doggie daddy.

Everyone nodded in agreement.

Her doggie mommy put her paws around her and gave her a big hug. "Just remember we'll always be in your heart. We share a special bond that can never be broken no matter how many miles separate us."

"Will you come visit me if I get sad?" The pug had tears in her big brown eyes.

"Yes! You can count on us to be there whenever you need us," said her doggie dad.

"You can use your postcards, and paw print stickers to send us a message," said Rocky.

The little pug was still a bit sad, but she felt much better knowing her family would visit her if she needed them.

Mrs. Barry strolled over to the pug family. "Is everything okay?"

"Arf, Arf!" they all replied.

"Great! It's time to cut the cake."

The little pug and her siblings ran over to the table which had a doggie cake and a human cake. Everyone sang "For He's A Jolly Good Fellow," and then they cut the cake. After the cake was devoured, everyone helped clean up, and then it was time to go. There were lots of hugs, and kisses and a few tears shed. Everyone agreed it was a great party.

CHAPTER 3

An Adventure in the Sky

The next morning the little pug and Julie got up nice and early, and Mrs. Barry drove them to the airport.

"Farewell, have a safe trip," said Mrs. Barry

"Thanks, Mrs. Barry," said Julie.

"Arf! Arf!"

"Okay, time for you to go in your doggie carrier," said Julie.

They went to the counter to drop off their luggage. The ladies at the counter took the bags and pointed them towards the security checkpoint. They walked passed dozens of small shops. The smell of warm ooey gooey treats wafted out the shops and filled their bellies. They walked past tons of stores until they found the correct location. Soon it was time to board the plane and fasten their seatbelts.

"As soon as the pilot turns off the seatbelt sign you can sit on my lap," said Julie turning towards to the little pug.

"Arf! Arf!" the pug replied.

Suddenly the engines rumbled, and the plane started down the run-way.

"Ladies and gentlemen, this is your captain speaking. "Please fasten your seatbelts and stay seated until the seatbelt light is turned off."

The little pug was excited and scared at the same time. The plane lifted off the ground, and the little pug could feel her ears popping. She remembered what her mommy told her and kept swallowing.

Finally, the popping stopped, and Julie was able to take her out of the doggie crate. The flight attendant gave her a small bowl of water and a tasty treat. For the rest of the flight, she sat on her mommy's lap and looked out at all the big fluffy clouds. Eventually, she drifted off to sleep and dreamt about her doggie family.

The little pug was chasing after her brother when she was suddenly shaken awake.

"Time to get back in your crate. We're going to be landing in a few minutes," said the flight attendant who was looking under the seats and making sure the overhead bins were closed.

As the plane descended the little pug felt butterflies in her tummy, and her ears began to pop again. Suddenly there was a big bump! The plane landed on the runway and came to a roaring stop. The little pug was happy to be getting off the plane and couldn't wait to see her new home.

CHAPTER 4

The New Home

Once they arrived in New York, they moved in with the Brown family because the pug's mommy, Julie had taken a job as a nanny.

The little pug and her mommy shared a big room, and they had plenty of space for all of their things. The house was actually outside of the city, so there was a big backyard for the little pug to run around and play.

There were two children named Mikey and Shelby, who gave the little pug lots and lots of attention. Sometimes it was too much attention, but then the little pug would just pretend to go to sleep. There was also a gray cat named Sheba, but she was not very friendly. Sometimes Sheba tried to scratch the little pug, so she stayed far away from this persnickety cat.

Although the little pug missed her old home, she did like this home because there was always lots of things to do. They had to drop off and pick up the kids from school and take them to soccer or baseball, depending on the day. It was quite fun, and the little pug made lots of new doggie friends, who sometimes were allowed to come for playdates.

One day the Barker family came to visit, and when they left they took the little pug puppy with them. The little puppy didn't know why this was happening. She wondered if she had done something wrong, and why her mommy didn't love her anymore. She thought about the times she was naughty and Julie scolded her. But she hadn't had an accident or chewed Julie's shoes in a very long time. And Julie always told her how much she loved her. She was very frightened.

 Her new mommy, Helen, told her that her old mommy, Julie, couldn't take care of her anymore, but that she did still love her very much. The little pug was sad. She missed everyone, and all she wanted to do was go home to her real parents. But she knew that wasn't possible, so she had to go and live with the Barker family.

CHAPTER 5

A Forever Home

The Barker family loved the little pug and treated her like a princess. Eventually, she began to feel comfortable. And although she missed both of her mommies, her new mommy Helen was the best mommy in the whole wide world. She also had a great daddy named George, two brothers named Brian and John, and a sister named Meaghan. There was even a bird named Chirpy. He tweeted all day long from inside a gigantic cage. Chirpy was green and very pretty, but she didn't know how to play, so the little pug didn't spend too much time with her.

Sometimes the little pug even ventured down to the visit the glass tank filled with fish that lived in the basement. The fish swam back and forth in the tank and sometimes they just stared at the pug.

While the little pug liked water, she couldn't quite figure out how to get into the glass tank nor did she understand "fish" talk. She decided to stick to the humans instead.

But even the humans were confusing. The little pug couldn't under-stand why the people went in and out so often, and she wondered where they went.

They said they were off to work or school and she wished she could go with them.

At the end of the day, they always returned and took care of the little pug. Sometimes they even took her with them to visit friends and family. Every day they took her out for long walks, and she got to know all the other puppies that lived on the block. Some of the puppies were nice, and some were mean, so she only played with the polite ones.

Sometimes Grandma and Grandpa Barker would come over to take care of her, and the little pug loved them very much. Grandma Barker would make her chicken livers, and Grandpa would take her for long walks. On Saturdays she would go to the dog park to visit her friends, and she would run around and jump and play for hours.

Because the little pug had moved around so much she was always a little bit afraid when she went for a ride in the car; sometimes she would cry. She loved her new family and hoped they would keep her forever, so she tried to be extra good.

The little pug always greeted her family with a happy arf when they returned home. She even learned how to bring her new daddy the newspaper.

"Thank you little one. You are truly the best little puppy in the entire world. We're so happy that you came to live with us."

"Arf! Arf!" the pug replied.

The little pug wagged her tail and sat by her daddy as he read the paper. When he finished reading the paper, he always spent time playing with her.

"I have a surprise for you," said Mommy Helen. She set up the laptop computer and pressed a few buttons.

The little pug was amazed when she looked at the screen and saw her doggie mommy and daddy. Her brother, Rocky was jumping up and down behind them. Mrs. Barry was even there waving hello!

"Mommy, Daddy, Rocky! I miss you all so much!"

"Are you okay? Mrs. Barry told us about your new family and we've been so worried."

"I was scared and sad, but now I'm happy. My new family is special. They all love me, and I love them, too."

They talked for another few minutes, and then it was time to say good-bye. Mrs. Barry said they would face chat again in a couple of weeks.

The little pug did a little dance. She was happy. Everything was perfect again.

CHAPTER 6

The Terrible Horrible Thing

Perfect that is until the most awful, terrible, horrible thing happened. A new black and white puppy, who was also very jumpy, came to live with the Barker family, too. Her name was Chewy, and she was the most annoying dog the little pug had ever met. She tried to eat the little pug's food and play with her toys. She never left the little pug alone. She would nip at her ankles, and push into her. The little pug tried to hide, but somehow Chewy always found her. The little pug was so sad. She didn't like this new puppy. The new puppy wasn't trained, and she kept making messes in the house. Nothing was the same, and the little pug didn't know what to do. She thought about running away, but she didn't even know how to cross the street and was afraid to go outside by herself. She tried to avoid Chewy as much as possible, especially after she heard the following conversation.

"Mom, we need to do something about Chewy. She's too wild, and she's always annoying my precious little puppy," said Meaghan.

The little pug loved her human sister. Meaghan always played with her and let her sleep in her princess bed.

"I agree," said John. "She keeps stealing my Hot Wheels." John was the youngest Barker child, and he played fetch with the little pug every day when he got home from school.

"I know, but we just need to give her some time to get adjusted," replied Mrs. Barker. "Maybe we should send one of them to stay with Grandma and Grandpa Barker for a little while."

The little pug jumped into Meaghan's lap and started to shiver.

Meaghan gave her a big hug.

"Don't worry you're staying right here."

"Let's see what happens. I don't think Grandma Barker would take Chewy; she's just too wild. Plus, Brian is very attached to her," replied Mrs. Barker. Brian was the oldest. He played Soccer and Chewy, and the pug helped him practice.

Now the little pug was scared. She loved Grandma and Grandpa, but she didn't want to move again. She liked her house, and she wanted things to go back the way they were before the intruder came to live with them.

CHAPTER 7

The Doctor's Visit

One day the little pug thought she would try to be nice to Chewy, so she brought some of her toys over, and they played for a little while. But then Chewy got mean, and Mrs. Barker separated them. The little pug heard Mrs. Barker say that they needed a crate to put Chewy into when she got wild. The little pug remembered her crate. She loved it, but now that she was older, it was no longer necessary. She preferred her nice fluffy bed, or at least, she used to before Chewy constantly laid on it.

The little pug wished she could move back with her doggie family. She didn't want to play anymore, so she just slept, and tried to avoid Chewy. She spent a lot of time hiding in Meaghan's room, or in the basement. She liked the bubble noises that came from the fish tank.

Today the little pug was frightened because she had to go to the veterinarian (doggie doctor) to get her shots. This was worse than spending the day with Chewy or taking a bath.

"Okay, little one, you're such a good little puppy," said Dr. Paul, "just one little pinch and we are done."

Dr. Paul looked over at Mommy, "How are things going with the new puppy?"

"Not very good," replied Mommy.

The little pug barked in agreement.

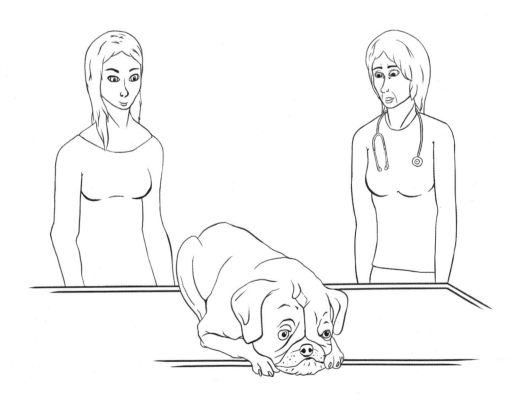

"Well, just give it some time, and everything should work out," said Dr. Paul.

"I hope so," said Mommy.

Me too, thought the little pug.

After the doctor's visit things seemed to be going better at home. The little pug felt happy. She could run around and eat and play without Chewy annoying her. Some days they even played together, and it was kind of fun. But there were still times when Chewy was too hyper and couldn't seem to control herself.

CHAPTER 8

The Dog Park

One day Mommy Helen took the little pug and Chewy to the dog park. The park had a big fence, so they didn't have to wear their leashes and could run all around with the other puppy dogs.

As soon as they got into the park, Chewy started taking the other doggies' toys. She was like a ping pong ball bouncing all over the place.

The little pug stayed close to the bench where her mother was sitting and played quietly with a few of her friends.

Suddenly a lady with curly red hair walked over to the bench. "Excuse me. Is that wild little doggie with you?"

"Yes, she is. Can I help you?" replied the little pug's mom.

"She's not playing nice and keeps taking everyone's toys. They don't mind sharing, but she is a bit too wild."

"I'm sorry, I'll speak to her right now. Chewy! Chewy!"

Chewy bounded over to the bench. "Chewy, I know you're having fun, but you need to calm down a bit, or we'll have to go home.

"Arf! Arf!" Chewy wagged her tail and sat down.

A little bit later she walked over to the little pug and tried to play with the other puppies. But they just ignored her. Then she tried to play with a bunch of bulldogs. She kept trying to play and suddenly Butch the bulldog pushed her away. Chewy went and sat in the corner by herself. The little pug was having so much fun with her friends that she didn't notice Chewy until she heard her crying.

"Whimper! Whimper!"

Chewy was surrounded by Butch the bulldog and his friends.

The little pug ran over to Chewy. "Arf! Arf! Arf! Grrr....grrr!" The little pug pushed the bulldogs away, and led Chewy back over to the bench by their mother. Mommy Helen gave them both a snack. They played together for a little bit longer, and then it was time to go home.

The little pug and Chewy got along much better after that day in the park. Sometimes Chewy was still very annoying, but the little pug just found a place to hide whenever Chewy got too wild.

One day when no one was home, the little pug and Chewy were having a game of tug of war. They were having the most fun they ever had running around the house and playing with different toys. The little pug felt so happy. It was nice to have someone to play with when the family went to work or school. But suddenly during a game of tug of war, the little pug felt a sharp pain in her eye.

CHAPTER 9

The Injury

"Ouch, that hurt," said the little pug.

"Sorry, sorry, sorry," said Chewy, "it was an accident."

"Okay! Hey, I didn't know you could talk," said the little pug.

"I didn't talk to you because I thought you didn't like me," said Chewy.

"I didn't, but you're okay, I guess. But my eye hurts, and I'm scared. I wish someone were home."

"Oh, no now I'm going to get in big trouble, and maybe they'll get rid of me like my other owners did," whimpered Chewy.

"I don't think they'll get rid of you. They're awfully nice, but you better learn how to behave."

CHAPTER 10

A Trip to the Vet

The next day the little pug went back to Dr. Paul, and he put some weird drops in her eye.

"Somehow you scratched the cornea of your eye, but you should be better in a couple of days."

The little pug didn't know what a cornea was, but she knew that it was part of her eye and that she was going to get better. But she did not like those eye drops, and wouldn't cooperate when she had to have them put in.

At first, the little pug's eye seemed to be getting better, but suddenly it got worse, so she had to go back to Dr. Paul. He checked her eyes and told Mommy Helen to give her new drops.

The little pug was getting upset. She didn't feel good, and she did not like these drops. They made everything look blurry. Every day she felt sicker and sicker, and she was getting very scared. Her eye was painful, and it made her cry. And when she dreamed about her doggie family she cried harder. She knew something was wrong because the entire family was upset, and Chewy was not allowed near her. But at least Chewy was not sent away, although the little pug did hear that they were thinking about sending Chewy to a new family. She wanted to tell her family that Chewy was now her friend and that it was an accident, but they didn't understand doggie language. She tried to think of a way to help Chewy, but she was just too tired. She spent most of her days sleeping.

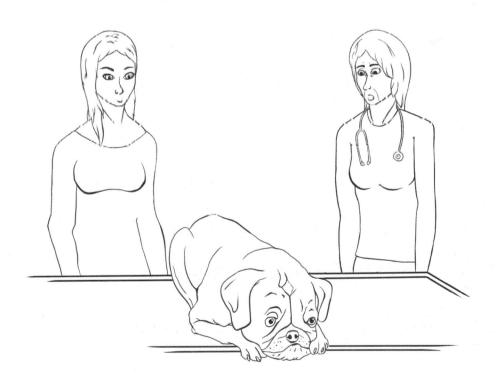

CHAPTER 11

The Operation

One day when the little pug woke up, she felt very sick. Her eye was very painful, and her mommy was crying. Everyone was very upset. The little pug was told she had to go to a hospital to be seen by a special doctor, who only took care of eyes. It was a very long ride, and she was frightened. Her family kept telling her she was going to be okay, and that they loved her.

When the little pug was taken into the special hospital, two doctors checked on her. They spoke to her mother who started to cry. The rest of the family just kept hugging the pug and telling her not to worry.

"This is a very serious issue, and we need to examine it more closely. She'll have to have an operation. We may not be able to save her eye," said Dr. Mary.

Operation! I don't want an operation, and I certainly don't want to lose my eye. I want to go home right now. I'm scared. Mommy is scared too, thought the little pug who tried to run out of the hospital room.

Her mother picked her up and gave the little pug a big hug. "Don't worry these nice doctors are going to help you get better. I love you."

"Yes, we all love you," everyone crowded around the little pug to give her a hug.

The two doctors took the little pug to another room, and they washed her and told her they were going to make her feel better. They explained that they were going to give her some medicine to help her fall asleep.

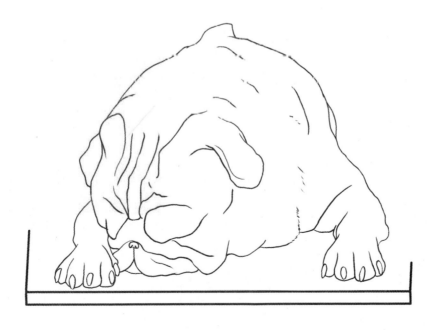

When the little pug woke up, she felt strange. At first, she didn't know where she was, but then she remembered the operation. She was dreadfully scared.

"I see you're finally awake," said Sally, the nurse. "Don't worry everything is going to be alright."

Dr. Mary stated, "The operation was a success, and you're going to feel better very soon. You're a brave little puppy."

The little pug had a big patch over her eye and a tube in her arm. She was so tired that she just fell back to sleep.

CHAPTER 12

The Road to Recovery

That night the little pug was still nervous. All night long doctors, and nurses came to check on her. They were nice to her, but they weren't her family. She wanted to go home and sleep in her own comfy bed. She felt strange because she could only see out of one of her eyes because something was covering the other one.

The next morning she felt a little better. Nurse Sally gave her some water to drink and a little bit of food, but she was still very tired.

At lunch time Dr. Mary came to check on the little pug. "You're such a brave little girl. Do you want to go outside for a walk?"

"Arf, Arf," the little pug wagged her tail.

"Okay, let's take the bandage off of your eye. It might seem a little strange at first, but you'll adjust."

Why can't I see out of my eye? the little pug thought to herself. She didn't understand why she couldn't open her right eye, and why she could only see out of her left eye.

After Dr. Mary finished taking off the bandage she put some cool liquid on it. "I know this is scary for you but in a few days you'll feel much better. Even though your eye is no longer there, you'll be able to see perfectly out of your other eye."

The little pug started to run around in circles and thought. *My eye is missing! Oh no, where did it go? Where is my mommy? I wish she were here.*

Dr. Mary picked up the little pug. "It's best not to get too excited. Let's go for a short walk. Your family will be here very soon to take you home."

Home! I'm going home. I must be okay if I'm going home. I can't wait to see everyone. At least I hope I can see them and they bring my stuffed bear and some treats, thought the little pug.

Dr. Mary took the little pug outside. At first, the sun hurt her eye, but soon she could see, and she ran all around the grass. She still had a little

bit of pain in her other eye but felt much better.

"What a brave little puppy you are," said Dr. Mary. "You still need to

take it easy. Let's go back inside, so you can get some

rest before your family comes to take you

home."

The little pug didn't want to go back

inside the hospital. She wanted to go

home, but she did feel kind of tired,

and soon she was in a deep sleep,

and dreamt about her family.

CHAPTER 13

Time to Go Home

"There's our little girl," the little pug was dreaming about her mother. The voice became louder, and the little pug felt someone rub her side. She opened her eye and was delighted to see her family gathered around her hospital bed. She jumped up and gave everyone a bunch of kisses.

The entire family was there. They were all laughing and crying. But they were happy tears. Dr. Mary and Nurse Sally explained the important things that needed to be done to help the little pug get better. She had to take special medicine, and her eyes had to be kept very clean. She also had to rest for a couple of days, and go back to the doctor in two weeks.

The little pug was so happy that she was finally going home. The car ride home was very long, and the little pug fell asleep.

"Time to wake up sleepy head, we're finally home," said Mommy.

Daddy carried her upstairs. Then Brian, Mcaghan, and John helped her get comfortable. They gave her some treats, her stuffed bear, and some water. They spread out a big blanket so they could all lie down on the floor together. The little pug looked around for Chewy, but she wasn't there.

"Wake up sleepy head," said Mommy. "We have a surprise for you."

The little pug jumped up and thought she would finally get to see Chewy, but the only thing she saw was the computer screen. Suddenly, she heard her doggie mommy's voice.

"Mommy! Mommy, I've been so scared. I kept dreaming of you."

"We've all been very worried, but Mrs. Barry assured us that you were going to get better."

The little pug spoke to her doggie family for a very long time. She told them all about Chewy and what had happened. She felt much better after she spoke to her family, but she still was worried about Chewy.

The little pug kept thinking. *Oh my, where is Chewy? I hope they didn't give her to another family. She didn't mean to hurt me. It was an accident. And I miss Chewy because she is my friend.*

Suddenly the little pug heard the doorbell ring. *Maybe that's Chewy.*

"Where is my little darling puppy?" said Grandma Barker. "You poor little thing."

Arf, Arf! *I am not a poor little thing, Grandma, I'm great. I wonder if Chewy is with Grandpa,* the little pug wondered.

"Look what Grandma has for you. I bought you a brand new bed."

Grandpa walked in with a brand new bed.

The little pug ran around in circles and thought. *Wow! A new bed! This is great. It's so soft and fluffy. And I love the color pink. If Chewy comes back, maybe I will let her sleep in it with me. I wish Chewy were here to see my new bed.*

CHAPTER 14

The Reunion

"Arf, Arf!"

Is that who I think it is? thought the little pug.

The little pug looked up just in time to see a flash of black and white whiz by her.

"You're still here. I was worried that they gave you up for adoption."

Chewy ran over to the little pug and licked her face. "I thought they were going to get rid of me, too. But I guess they do love me. Are you okay? What happened to your eye?"

"I'm okay. I had to have an operation, and now I only have one eye, but I can see pretty well. And Grandma bought me a cool new bed," said the little pug.

"I got a new bed, too, but I also have a crate. I have to go in my crate when no one is home, so I don't hurt you again. I wouldn't hurt you on purpose, but I do get excited. I missed you, and I'm sorry about your eye."

"Thanks, I know you wouldn't hurt me on purpose. I used to have a crate, and I loved it."

"It's not so bad as long as I don't have to stay in it too long. And now that you're home I won't be so lonely when everyone leaves," said Chewy.

"Chewy, leave the little pug alone she needs to rest," said Grandma.

The little pug and Chewy both went to lie down in their new beds, and soon they were both snoring.

Time went by, and each day the little pug felt better, and all the other dogs and even some of the cats were nicer to her; at least for a couple of weeks. Chewy began to calm down and didn't get in too much trouble; at least not as much as before. Everything was back to normal; at least until the day Chewy ran away, but that's a tale for another day.

If you haven't figured it out yet, my name is Lola, and this is my story. And I don't want you to feel sorry for me because I'm just perfect. And I get lots of attention from everyone because now I'm Lola the One Eyed Pug, and I'm even more special to my family.